MORE ADVENTURES OF WEE ROBERT BRUCE

Dumbarton Rock and Other Stories

By Paul V Hunter
Illustrations by Anne Marshall
and Catherine Crome

AUCH ✦ BOOKS

First Published in 2014
Text copyright © Paul Hunter
Photographs copyright © Paul Hunter
Illustrations copyright © Anne Marshall/Catherine Crome

First published in Scotland 2014 by
Auch Books, Bonhill, West Dunbartonshire, Scotland
www.auchbooks.co.uk

British Library catalogue record for this book is
available from the British Library.

ISBN 978-0-9536316-4-3

Book design and artwork by Sarah Crome
Illustrations by Catherine Crome and Anne Marshall
Cover design by Sarah Crome
Printed in Scotland by Anderson Printers, Govan, Glasgow

Acknowledgements

I have dedicated this second book in the 'Wee Bruce' series, to all children. They are more than our future - they are our inspiration. Profits from the sale of the first edition of this book will be given to *Yorkhill Children's Charity* - the fundraising body for Yorkhill Hospital, Glasgow. There is a very personal and special connection to this place, not least because one of our illustrators, twelve-year-old Catherine Crome, has been receiving treatment for cancer here.

Yorkhill's Shiehallion Ward is a place where children are given hope in the fight against cancer. I would like to recognise the unseen work and dedication from all the staff who work here and who have taken such good care of Catherine. Because of this, her future looks bright.

So with this in mind, I would like to acknowledge Catherine Crome for inspiring me with her super human strength during her fight against a terrible desease for someone so beautiful and young. Her wonderful chapter heading illustrations really do draw the reader in to each story.

Once again, young Connor Pollock has been our star 'wee Bruce' and our friend, Elke Spitzer, has provided excellent support on the final stages of production.

To Sarah Crome, my friend and publisher, once again I have to thank for all her hard work and organisation under extreme and exeptional circumstances with Catherine's treatment. Not only has she been there for her two daughters, dealing with day to day family duties, but she has been able to bring about this second book which, without her, would still be on my computer.

To Anne Marshall, I would like to give thanks as an amazing artist. Fate brought us together and she has really used her talent to bring my book to life with her superb pen and ink illustrations. She has patiently listened to Sarah and me with our crazy ideas and recreated the scenes with real flair and vision.

Finally, I would like to recognise the Brothers Grimm of Germany for their fantastic imagination in the telling of folklore and fairy tales. For the last two hundred years, they have influenced writers and filmakers with stories that have captivated readers and audiences around the world.

Thank you for your awakening.

Paul V Hunter
June 2014

Contents

Page

9   1. Dumbarton Rock

32   2. The Burn

56   3. Maid

73   4. Fever

93   About the author

94   About the illustrators

96   Also from Auch Books

I.

DUMBARTON ROCK
by Paul V Hunter

Dumbarton Rock

Today was going to be a special day for wee Bruce and his friend. They were spending the winter's day and night at Dumbarton Rock, a castle older than time itself. Forgotten peoples from the past lived here at one time; including Picts, Celts and Vikings and there was nowhere else more haunted than here. For a thousand years many battles and conflicts were fought over this huge lump of frozen volcano and many a person lost their lives inside these castle walls. Some were even thrown over the wall to a very high death fall or they were simply thrown down the well. There were stories of captured prisoners being tortured and never to be seen again once they stepped through the massive gates. It

was full of activity and was a maze of dark seedy corners, shadowy walkways and dark places to hide. It was a child's playground.

A banquet was being held for all the princes, princesses and nobles alike to celebrate Christmas, and that meant wine, merriment, song and dancing. The children were encouraged to go off and play within the safety of the ancient fortress, so wee Bruce and Malcolm Lennox did just that. Their first port of call was to investigate all the out-houses and availability of gaining entry to the dungeons; a dark place off limits to most people. First building to give a wide berth was the castle chapel. There was no interest there, only interfering oldies. Rising into the heavens from the great hall was a set of steps, stopping at the portcullis, a huge metal and wooden protective gate that was lowered down to protect the upper part of the castle itself. Once the gate was down there was no way of entering unless you fancied an arrow in your chest or a pot of boiling oil poured over your head from above in the guard house.

With a duet chorus of heavy breathing, the boys climbed the stairs and stopped at the portcullis.

From above came the voice of a guard,
"What do you want?"
"We would like to gain entry, good Sir," replied wee Bruce.
"By whose authority?" asked the man.
"I don't know. We just want to have some fun. My father's eating in the great hall."

"I'm just pulling your leg son, c'mon in but don't get up to no good and stay safe, don't go near the wall edges."

Malcolm answered, "We won't, Sir, we going on an adventure."

"An adventure?" laughed the man. "Then you have to visit the shoemaker Nuggle Succabus, go up the first set of stairs and turn left, you'll maybe find him there."

The huge gate creaked and sprang into action. Clanging metal and the noise of machinery echoed all through the upper castle. Inch by inch the bulk of defence lifted off the ground and stopped after a few feet leaving enough space for the boys to sneak under. Once through, the massive metal structure dropped onto the cobbled ground, resulting in an enormous thud as it came down, giving the boys their first fright of the night. They sprinted up the next set of stairs.

Attached to the walls were lit torches, wood wrapped in binding and soaked in animal fat, so seeing where they were going was no problem. Coming up on their right side was a small dungeon. They didn't get too close but heard the rattling of chains and the sounds of someone making a splash sound with their feet. A rat squeezed through the space between the bars and ran off in the other direction holding onto something between its teeth. From above their heads came the noise of animals in their pens. A cow

gave off a moo, which set off a sheep, which set off a pig
grunting and finally set off the chickens clucking in panic.

The boys backed away from the noise, passing by the main
dwellings, they came to a stop at a small stone shelter.
Moving in close together the young heroes walked to the
entrance. Not wanting to rush in, they stepped forward
almost in a slow soft motion, giving their eyes time to
accustom to the dark.

"You won't find anyone in there," said a voice.

From the shadows stepped forward a small man wrapped
in sack cloth. They couldn't see his face, but the dim light
from the moon was enough to see lips moving to the voice.
His lips were very blue.

"That's not where you want to go, gentlemen Sirs, can I
tempt you in travelling to a place where mortal man does
not dwell? To enter a place not of this world and lose
yourselves in a the caverns of mythology, forget where you
come from or where you are going and open your minds
to the unthinkable, unstinkable and unsinkable…Well, are
you up to the task?"

"What is it you want?" asked Malcolm.

"For goodness sake," replied the man, "do you want to
participate in the said supernatural happenings? Adventure,
gentleman Sirs, a happening!"

"Okay," said wee Bruce, "what do we have to do? We don't

have any money."

"Insult me not, Sirs, with the talk of money. Instead, go forward from here and search out the huge stone slab shaped like a mushroom. Wait until the moon is cloudless and touch the stone with your big toe and thumb. Tell them Nuggle Succabus sent you; the shoemaker; the keeper of the door that's not there."

"Does it matter if our big toes are not clean?" asked Malcolm.

"Go now, young lads, before the moon hides for the night and you lose your chance of touching the netherworld," insisted the man, urging the boys onwards. "Go, go quickly and don't forget … don't take anything that doesn't belong to you."

The boys made their way forward, walking closer as if they were joined at the hip.

"Do you think he's crazy?" asked Malcolm, "He's obviously a madman."

Wee Bruce searched the walls with his eyes, "I don't know, he seemed to know what he was talking about even if we didn't understand most of it."

Music and singing could be heard from the great hall below, echoing upwards through every nook and cranny in the castle, bouncing off the walls as it travelled its course. The temperature at the higher part of the castle had dropped and there was a definite chill in the air. The boys were willing to go anywhere to get out of the cold so they continued forward in their search for the stone slab shaped like a mushroom.

"Did the man say what kind of mushroom?" asked Malcolm.

Wee Bruce shrugged his shoulders, "I don't know, a mushroom's a mushroom I suppose, does it really matter what kind it is?"

"It matters to our gardener, he's always shoving mushrooms in front of my face trying to explain dozens of different ones. Let's go back and get him, he'll know and ..." Wee Bruce stopped him in mid-sentence. "Now there's something that looks like a mushroom."

They both looked upwards and there in front of their eyes was a huge fungi shaped from solid rock. It was massive

and quite overpowering in stature and gave off the feeling of foreboding, sending a shiver of uncertainty up their young spines. The two boys stood silent and dwarfed in the company of a giant mushroom.

"Wow…right," said Malcolm, "this is it, socks off…"
They both threw themselves to the ground pulling their boots and socks off. Sitting together they flung an arm around each other's shoulder and placed the soles of their feet onto the cold hard lifeless rock, pushing hard on their big toes. With arms extended they placed both dirty thumbs in front of the stone.

"Well?" said wee Bruce, "this is it."
"Do we go for it?" asked Malcolm. "Are we brave enough?"
After looking at each other in the eye for a moment, the boys pressed forward, thumbing the stone. There was silence. They waited. And waited.

Just as it seemed they were sitting there forever, a small door, big enough to crawl through, slid open, making the noise of two heavy boulders rubbing together. The boys couldn't believe it. Wee Bruce flung himself head first into the space with Malcolm following straight after him. They were in. But in where? No sooner after they entered, the door closed behind them. There was no way back now.

It was dark to begin with, but after a few seconds it was as if someone lit thousands of torches. The walls seemed to be built of crystal, magnifying light a million times, it was nature's own way of creating daylight. They were in a very large and deep cavern built into the inside of the castle itself. There were chambers upon chambers upon chambers going in all directions with tunnels carved into the rock leading left, right, upwards and downwards. It was a mesmerising, fantastic, crystal room. And yet it was warm enough. There was no wind or draft and the whole inside seemed to be heated by a nice warm glow, warm enough to encourage the growth of inner trees. Decorated on the sides of the chamber were ancient giant willow and yew trees, decorated at the bases by a million umbrellas of fungi, the roots grasping onto them like tight fisted hands and painted in all colours of shady reds and purples, giving the impression of autumn.

Our adventurers decided to take the route downwards, following a set of carved out marble stairs leading deeper into the chamber. On the descent, the boys' hands ran over wall carvings depicting scenes from old, with warriors slaying dragons and mythical beasts crashing onto ships. Higher upon the walls, hand prints encased in blood red paint pointed the way to the next level and they could do nothing but obey. But there was more to follow as a bigger surprise awaited them, there was noise coming from deep down and it seemed to sound as if someone or something

was moving around. The boys slowed their steps and walked
on their tiptoes so not to give away their presence. Not
noticing a shaded sharp short shard of marble, Malcolm
placed the sole of his foot upon it and screamed out with
all his might. The noise echoed twenty times as loud
throughout the whole underground chamber, forcing the
boys to place their hands over their ears.

"Now you've done it," whispered wee Bruce.

"But something stabbed into the bottom of my foot,"
whispered Malcolm in return, "I thought it was a dragon
biting me, look, it's bleeding."

"So a dragon just happened to be sitting on the step
waiting for someone to bite, did it?" argued wee Bruce.

From below cried out a voice. "Who's there? Come out
and show yourself."

The boys froze on the spot, then slowly retreated back up another step. Malcolm let out another scream, "I've stood on it again, oh my poor foot!"

"Come down and show yourself I say," repeated the voice. The boys had no choice but to step downward and show themselves, they couldn't exactly hide now as they had given themselves away in the biggest way possible.

Stepping down Bruce lost his balance, he held onto Malcolm, he lost his balance and leaned onto Bruce, both fell down tumbling to the flat ground below in a heap.

"Glad you could make it," said the voice. "C'mon in, make yourselves at home."

Climbing onto their feet the boys looked around but couldn't see anyone there.

"Hello?" asked wee Bruce. "Where are you?"

"I'm up here," answered the voice.

"Up where?" said Malcolm.

"We got lost, we're trying to find our way out", fibbed wee Bruce.

"Nobody manages to find this place by accident," remarked the voice.

"It was Nuggle Succabus's fault. He sent us," stuttered Malcolm. "He made us come in. We didn't want to come in but he forced us …"

"When I get my hands on that little weasel I'm going to pull his arms and legs off," screamed the voice. "You better

not be after my ruby diamond."

"Sir," said wee Bruce trying to explain, "we're not interested in any diamond, honestly, we're just looking for an adventure."

The boys sat down on a huge rounded stone, rubbing their sore bits from the fall. Suddenly the huge stone under them moved throwing them back onto the ground. They just happened to be sitting on the biggest foot they'd ever seen. They looked up and looking down on them was a giant woman.

"Oh, by the way don't call me Sir, I'm a Lady," she said.

A huge woman who they thought was part of the cave stood up and peered down at the two tiny boys. She was wearing a massive chainmail skirt, big enough to be used as a sail on a boat, a leather studded sleeveless top showing bigger muscles than of any man and a huge nose piercing. Her hair was darker than rusty metal, her four toed feet were flat and broad with black toenails and her long arm skin gave a rubbery appearance and was covered in hair. From her wrists were fastened beautiful ornate silver and gold bracelets and most amazing of all was in her belly button. Inside sat the biggest, shiniest, glittering red ruby ever seen by man. It was stunning.

"My name is Stalag the Mite. This is my home and I've lived here for over one thousand and three hundred years, three hundred and forty five days and seventeen hours."
"How did you get here and how did you manage to get actually inside?" asked wee Bruce.
"And what do you do if you want to go outside?" asked Malcolm.
"I don't," she said, "I'm trapped here, have been ever since I was put under a sorcerers spell. I was trapped here by the Romans, then the Picts and Celts, then once the well dried up the Vikings left, leaving me here alone. Once the Vikings left there was a huge heavy humongous hail and rain storm and the wells filled back up again. I am of the world of

forgotten. Here I am the Queen of nowhere. I serve my sentence of heartache and invisibility from the world and imprisoned until my secret release is found. Until then I am shackled for an eternity to this fossilised graveyard. "

She bowed her head down low towards the boys. "You sure you're not here just to steal my ruby? Cause if you were I'd crush your bones just like the others."

"Others?" asked wee Bruce.

She pointed over to a corner of the cave. Sitting piled up on high were the bones and armour of countless soldiers and warriors who tried to take her red ruby diamond.

"Many have come and tried and many have failed, because there is no man or army strong enough to defeat Stalag the Mite!" she boasted.

"What do you do with yourself in your cave since you can't leave?" asked wee Bruce.

"I juggle," she answered.

Both boys asked at the same time, "Juggle what?"

"Bones, stones, water and spit balls if I'm bored enough."

Again she pointed to another corner in the cave and it was stacked high with rolled up balls of spit, held together by lines of phlegm.

"Where did you get so much spit?" asked Malcolm.

"From people," she answered, "a thousand years of people spitting it away down through the cracks and ending up in my cave. Would you like some?"

Between them, the boys couldn't decide who was going to throw up first.

"If a spell was put on you then surely it can be taken away?" asked wee Bruce.

The giant explained that she racked her brain every single day since she was trapped, wondering how to rid the spell, but she could never figure it out so gave up years ago.

"I have to sleep now, but not for long," she said. "Since I've been entombed here the air and crystals have changed my blood and I become very sleepy. If I don't get enough sleep I want to crush bones." She closed her eyes and became part of the cave once more. As the boys sat quiet wondering what their next move should be, a single eye opened and she spoke, "Don't get any ideas; don't touch anything; don't go snooping around... I won't be long." The eye closed.

"What do you think, Malcolm?" asked wee Bruce in a whisper.

Malcolm didn't answer, his eyes were fixed on the ruby stone stuck comfortably in her giant belly button. His gaze was fixed at this sparkling gem. He couldn't pull himself away from leering at it. He was mesmerised and in a trance state.

Wee Bruce couldn't believe it. "What you doing?"

Malcolm answered with his gaze still fixed tight on the splendid jewel, "Have you ever seen anything so amazingly wonderful? I must have it."

"Look around you at all the bones, they thought it looked amazingly wonderful, too, until they were crushed under one of her spit balls. These weren't boys like us, they were fierce warriors armed to the teeth and experienced fighters," stated wee Bruce.

"But I know I can get it," snapped Malcolm.

Without a hint of his next move Malcolm leapt forward like a boy possessed and ran straight towards the sleeping giant. Wee Bruce threw his hands on his head in astonishment and stepped back, aiming his body towards the exit. Malcolm climbed up nearby rocks getting himself within belly button height. He looked back at wee Bruce who was waving his arms and shaking his head. Raising himself up in his bare feet he grappled at the ruby, digging his way through piles of belly button fluff and forcing it out of the giant's belly, then turned and jumped a good way down to the rock floor. As he hit the floor the ruby flew out of his hands and landed way in front of him, spinning like a top.

The giant's eyes opened, moving away from the rock face she screamed out in anger and leaned forward in the boy's direction. Wee Bruce ran back picking up the ruby, helping Malcolm up to his feet and both of them headed for the way out in super speed fashion. Before they knew it, massive balls of spit were crashing off the walls near to them, one half soaking Malcolm as they disappeared up another tunnel. They ran for what their lives were worth. Further up they stopped as they knew the giant was too big to come after them.

"I can't believe you did that, are you crazy?" yelled an out of breath wee Bruce.

"I knew I could get it," said Malcolm, "I told you so didn't I?"

"You… we could have been killed, you idiot!" screamed wee Bruce.

"But we didn't, can't you see, we got the ruby, we got the ruby ha, ha, ha," laughed Malcolm.

"Let's just get out of here before she finds a way of getting to us, I think she's going to be pretty angry and I don't plan to have my bones crushed or taken out by a huge spit ball wrapped in phlegm."

They followed the sign of the red hands back to where they entered and stood at the entrance.

Just as the boys thought they were safe, the giant pulled off her toe nails and flung them through the tunnel. Bits of thick black nails crashed into the walls around them, splitting into thousands of small pieces and getting tangled in their hair.

"So, what do we do now, how do we get out of here?" urged wee Bruce.

"It must be the same toe and thumb secret we used to get in," replied Malcolm.

They both sat on the ground and pressed their big toes against the rock. Wee Bruce sat the ruby to the side as they gently pushed their thumbs against the entrance. They waited. Nothing happened. They shifted their feet a couple of times and tried again, but to no avail.

"It's no use, we're stuck in here." wee Bruce cried.

"We'll probably rot in here with her back there, and we'll grow as bitter as she is after a thousand years of doing nothing but juggle spit balls. I'm afraid I've really done it this time," moaned Malcolm. He dropped his head and looked to the ground. He was hating himself for really messing it up big time. In the background the giant was screaming in bursts of anger and vexing her displeasure by snarling and gnarling to herself, by grinding her teeth and stamping her feet. She would stand on one leg and kick the walls with the other, making her blood boil even more than it was. She was infuriated, exasperated and enraged. She wasn't a happy puppy.

Malcolm picked up the ruby. "Have you ever seen anything so beautiful? This could have changed our worlds forever.

We could have been the richest men in the Kingdom."
The diamond sparkled in his eyes, lighting up his face. He
pressed it against his lips and kissed it. "Oh magnificent
diamond, it could have been so different. Many brave men
have fought to steal your beauty and lost; now there is no
place for you, not even a belly button." He passed it on to
wee Bruce who held it closely to his face and marvelled at
its mirrored colours. Intoxicated, he kissed its beauty, too.
All of a sudden there was a blinding flash and the ruby was

gone. It completely vanished from his hands and was no more. Malcolm jumped back in surprise and wee Bruce just sat with his empty hands open. Then hidden door slid open to the side.

The giant fell silent. The boys didn't know what to think. The screams of rage from the giant changed to screams of joy and she sounded as if she was really close to them. There was laughing and singing and a loud yippee thrown everywhere.

Instead of disappearing out the door, they sat as the giant turned the corner next to them. Standing in front of them was a girl. She was normal height and was overjoyed, running past the boys and squeezing out the entrance to the real chilly world outside.
"I'm free," she shouted, "I'm free after all these years, I'm back! Oh, the wonderful smell of fresh air, the sky, the grass and the hills … yippee!" She danced a merry dance and skipped her way into the darkness, disappearing out of site. The boys looked at each other and said nothing. What had broken the spell?

Nuggle Succabus appeared outside. "You going to stay in there forever?" he asked.
The boys stepped outside and with that, the sliding stone door closed on the cavern for good, never to open again.

"What was that all about?" asked wee Bruce. "What did we just see in there?"

"You broke the spell, gentleman Sir," said Nuggle Succabus, "You freed her after an eternity trapped in a stone hell, she is now free to wonder the world at her leisure."

Wee Bruce was curious, "But she says she was going to crush your bones, why would she say that?"

He explained, "I promised her I would find her a way out years ago and she never forgot. She thought I had forgotten and left her to rot in a world of loneliness but I couldn't free her because I didn't know how."

Malcolm still didn't understand. "You mean all anyone had to do was to kiss the ruby twice and the spell was broken? Surely men have kissed its beauty before?"

"No, not that simple," he said. "The ruby had to be kissed by a future king who knew nothing of the stone. That was the only way to break the spell, so you, gentleman Sir, must be a true king in the making, otherwise the spell would not have been broken."

With that, the man walked away and vanished into the darkness never to be seen.

The boys made their way back down the steps towards the portcullis.

"Well?" shouted the guard. "Found any ghosts?"

"No," answered wee Bruce, "we bumped into your friend Nuggle Succabus, he told us where to go to find an adventure."

The guard's face turned whiter than white. "You mean you really saw Nuggle Succabus? He died years ago and his ghost is supposed to return every moonlit night to try and free his giant sister, who was locked inside a cave by the Picts for spitting like a demon. Her body was never found and he still haunts the place to this day, so don't go poking fun at old Nuggle."

"Well, I don't think he'll be bothering anyone again," said wee Bruce.

The guard hauled the gate high enough for the boys to squeeze under and bid them a goodnight. "Don't have nightmares tonight," he laughed.

Wee Bruce and Malcolm never discussed their adventure with anyone since that day and every time they get together at a full moon, they always wondered about Dumbarton Rock being special. Malcolm knew wee Bruce was special.

THE END

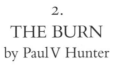

2.
THE BURN
by Paul V Hunter

The Burn

Wee Bruce sank into the depths of sleep. Sinking deeper and deeper. Free falling into emptiness. Forever falling, cascading downwards with stomach butterflies rambling upwards.

His journey's end was the Bannock burn, a small winding, mudded river near Stirling Castle. He became aware of his dream as his invisible status landed him dead centre in one of the deadliest battles of medieval times. The experience of war would be a terrible lesson of man's brutality to himself, but as the boy had witnessed both death and suffering in his young life, this was different. To kill an animal to eat was one thing – to see man taking a man's life just to stub out his existence was another.

Unfortunately for the boy, his vantage point belonged in a privileged seat in the front row of the theatre of dark destruction. He would endure first-hand experience from the realm of safety. It was his vision to see, and visually participate in the dynamic presentation, and although bereft of choice he was chosen to witness it. It was war.

A multitude of warriors filled the eye line as far back in the horizon. Wee Bruce began to process the images sent to him. It was destruction married with carnage and mayhem with sweaty men and beasts becoming the norm of the day. Dressed to kill, intermingled brethren shook hands with death and cheaply parted with their shattered mortal bodies. The destruction of the human race seemed paramount as the butcher's market was open for business. The deafening sound of metallic contact was followed by screams and foul language delivered between both sets of warriors, with teeth, bones and tabards swirling around, drawn by the magnet of the eye of the storm.

Carpets of damaged corpses began to fill up to knee depth as the battle meat grinder prepared its skirmish of the day. Shields displaying their lattice battle scars began to mount up and sliced infantry lay grasping open wounds, unable to move or react towards the slaughter surrounding them. They remained silent, accepting their fate into the hands of God as they prayed for a quick end, rather than a slow agonising nightmare.

Wee Bruce covered his eyes but thousands of faces looked
back at him. It was too much to take in for a young boy.
Riders feet trapped by harnesses, were dragged into the
distance and hunted by axe wielding followers aiming to
finish them off.

Nature was hurting too, as veered carpets of grass and
nettles were spoiled by the war horses stamping in defiance.
Spills of thrown horseshoes littered the entrance to the
burn, hours of blacksmith hammering going to waste as
patches of purple crowned thistles lay flattened, life crushed
from their spiked stocks. On the opposing side of the
burn lay dead armies of cloaked white helmeted hogweed,
their summer
was over for
another year.

Just as wee
Bruce thought
the volume of
noise couldn't
get any
louder, new
momentum arrived in the distance, as choruses of crowd
roars hung in the air, echoing back and forth.

Out of range, contact continued with war horses and
columns of spear men standing as giant hedgehogs, clashing
head on, throwing explosions of dust and dirt skywards.
Flags and banners of all persuasions snapped and toppled,
trampled underfoot never to be looked upon again. Clean
white surcoats changed colour immediately, as blood, sweat
and dark earth diluted the family heraldry. Above, the blue
sky never faltered as the odd cloud blocked the sun and

presented shade for a short spell to the masses of hacking infantry below. The world around wee Bruce struggled to breathe.

The beasts of burden were dragged into man's weakness to kill. These beautiful noble creatures once roamed the world's plains in peace and for a millennia survived under God's law of nature. Now forced into man's shameful world, they screamed in disapproval as their eyes bulged outwards from fear and the struggle to understand. They hurled their riders like human missiles, somersaulting their tin men into the air in refusal to cross the burn.

Although horsemeat was a delicacy of the time, there would be no feast at the table today, for their guests would be the sun baked maggot and bluebottle. Maimed horses lay still, awaiting their un-deserved fates. Cries of "On them!" sounded through the mess as at last came a breakthrough in the onslaught of hell. Pockets of silence fell around groups of marauding skirmishers and at last individual commanders voiced their orders to attack more and more, taking advantage of the hard earned ground.

One single solitary rowan tree became a focal point and safety blanket for many a loose horse sheltering from killer man. Wee Bruce was witnessing the era when man traded his youth against the skills of the art of combat. From

boy to man, it was an apprenticeship in how to wound or kill an opponent, all under the name of chivalry. The boy saw nothing noble or regal in death, and as the fight was coming to a climax it was becoming uglier.

In the distance, Stirling Castle towered above everything else. This was the prize awaiting the invaders if they won the day. It glowed from the array of lit torches as the sheriff used the great height as the perfect vantage point to witness the feast on this day of 'John the Baptist'.

At the water's edge, the burn came alive, opening its mouth to swallow up as many fleeing soldiers as it could during a muddy feeding frenzy. Men sank under the tidal water, their hands grappling at the surface fighting for breath. Scared desperate screams were ignored, muted and unheard by the mass of orchestrated horse farts. Adding insult to injury, weapons rained down on them, quickening the journey to the after-life.

From the devilish turmoil came a telling and heart rending sight. Statued in the middle of the battlefield stood a boy about wee Bruce's age. He wore no armour or chainmail, carried no weapons of war, and trapped between his arm and face towered a banner pole. The flag hung still. There were no telling signs of wounds or injury, it just appeared as if the poor tragic boy had seen enough and had given up.

Just as wee Bruce thought he'd had enough, from the king's position on high, horns sounded out strategy and instruction. Imitating a larger-than-life chess board, knights and pawns crossed the grasses in mass ranks to confront each other with checkmate in mind.

Then, from the low depths appeared a dark mysterious harbinger of devilish woes. Just like wee Bruce, the gathered masses were unaware of this mystic storyteller of doom as she began her spiel.

"Dance your contorted dance, brave tin soldiers."
She outstretched her bony finger and pointed to the boy.
"With rival athletic bodies, they will break dance their bloody graffiti artists and paint violent opposition. I will reach you a crescendo of vulgar and sinful pirouettes partnered by frolicking embraces."
She twisted her body towards wee Bruce, pressing her nose against his.
"I am the bringer and deliverer of the end times and I hunger for the banquet of destruction and turmoil for which I thrive and multiply in my place of misery and loss."
Carrying a wry smile, she faded down into her ground.

Then all changed. Wee Bruce was spared the ongoing relentless meat grinding battle. A feeling of immunity came over him and he could observe the war from a new vantage point. He found himself placed within a tent, facing a lonely figure of a man sitting at an even lonelier table, his head placed on the table top as if asleep. He wore slightly dusted shoulder armour, the dulled chrome disturbed by a weapons contact, disfiguring the image of a lion rampant. His red and gold surcoat hung loose enough exposing his chainmail shirt, advertising missing links and rust, nestled on his finger shone a ring … a king's ring.

His fists of dirt accompanied by black chipped fingernails branched upon huge hands, were hardened and tempered by many a skirmish and bitter winter's night guerrilla tactics. Not far from his reach lay a wooden Celtic designed shaft, bereft of its polished axe head, the sharp end sat divorced, rendered useless by a human skull and now a shattered ornament.

The oak lined table top, soaked up the sweat and wetness from his dark brown hair, its length flowing longer than most men of his age alongside loose wavy curls of plenty. As if the King was aware of the boy's presence, he sat straight backed on his creaking, elongated chair and presented his full profile. For a brief spell he seemed to stare at wee Bruce, his gaze finally broken when another presence entered the tent. Glancing clean through the boy dominated an almost pious and ordained bearded facial powerhouse.

Scribed behind dark circled eyes shone an intelligence and a deep understanding about life. Owing to a jousting accident in his youth, running from the tip of his forehead gorged a scar, coming to an end and buried deep in his facial hair. He was handsome in a rugged sort of way. From behind an overgrown multi coloured moustache displayed uneven teeth and bold heavily dry cracked lips. His skin was well beaten by weather, almost touching on a Moorish dark brown leather quality.

His brow was over bearing, helping to mask deep set eyes splashed with slightly blood shot veins. His head was in proportion to his six foot large frame, which upon stood an overdeveloped neck fit for a lion. Yet behind the full mane sat a man with his heart set deep in his country's liberty and existence. He'd sacrificed all and it hung in his eyes like trophies. Then it was all change again.

The boy found himself queuing in front of a huge bed. The room stank of incense, forcing the more sensitive of visitors to retch and presenting them with an excuse to leave the tension of the room.

There wasn't much light, only a few candles were lit and the reflected glare had misplaced its sparkle in illuminating the room. Lying neck deep in warm covers, lay a still figure of a man who'd been something important and special in their lives. A quiet chorus of sobbing and whimpering was played over and over again, broken only by noses being emptied into perfumed handkerchiefs.

Both men and women bowed their heads in hurt, and not shy in expressing their emotions, took it in turn to speak softly into his ear to remind him of their loyalty and undying love. All positions from regal to lords closed ranks as one family, helping to build strength and support for each other in coming to terms with their imminent heart breaking loss. In a way, wee Bruce was privileged, not many boys his age had witnessed the death of a king.

Like a freezing mist manoeuvring around tall trees, he too glided effortlessly forward to the front of the mourners. There before him was the regal man he'd witnessed earlier. Here, there were no signs of wound or blood loss. He was physically decaying and worn to the bone. His vinyl brown hair colour had become a matt grey. With his bone structure peaking more prominent, his eyes were lost behind white bushing eyebrows. His skin had become a transparent blue-grey tone, mouth slightly open throwing out gentle breaths, making it difficult to know if he was breathing at all.

Then without warning, his eyes opened slightly, causing an uproar and little relief to those giving respects. From the recess of dark eye sockets, he focused on the boy and as he struggled to speak, he produced softly spoken words.

"I see you," he said, "I know you and you know me - we are one."

Wee Bruce stepped back, causing the king's gaze to follow him. Unbeknown to the others, the old man's actions were perceived as fever madness and a few stepped forward to reassure him. The king never lost his focus on the boy.

"Dear Robert, we were wise, "We knew the truths about our path in life and we sacrificed all for Scotland."

He coughed a little, an aid placed a wet cloth to his heavily cracked dark lips, "This time and place has sucked the life from us ... return to the forests and lose yourself in spirit." As his head sank deep into the pillow of comfort, he managed to spit out his last remaining words.

"I see you, Robert ... I see me."

From nowhere stepped forward a young boy, the King's son, he was a mirror image to wee Bruce but younger. The dying Lord placed a hand on to his son's head, consoling the youngster as the toddler cried his heart out. The gathered group was emotionally and collectively broken. Princes, princesses, knights and minions wept as a single tear ran down the great man's cheek, the wetness stopping and settling in an old battle scar. Outside, packs of dogs screamed into the air, hailing the coming news to all around.

A handsome, well-built knight came forward, wearing a partly blue surcoat fixed with three white stars. Very carefully he placed a decorative sword of golden importance at his master's side. He kneeled to his lord, gripping his hand tight and resting his face on the tired twisted fingers. To hear such a stalwart warrior sob uncontrollably was disturbing and soul destroying, his chest heaving and his other hand twisting at the bed sheet in anger and disbelief. He failed miserably to hide his love with tears, displaying last respects worthy of any man.

Young ladies hovering at the back were helped out of the room, once again the smell of incense escaping with them as the door was opened. Outside in the hall steps, sat maids and house workers, inconsolable, hugging each other and stopping to give prayer.

From above the dim candle-lit chamber, appeared a glowing ball of light floating above the bed, immediately illuminating the King's face. No-one in the chamber was aware of its brilliance, and as it descended lower, wee Bruce watched in amazement as the old man's spirit was plucked away from the lifeless body, vacating years of pain and suffering. He was free.

Many of the shadowed spectators dropped to their knees in prayer, the remainder left standing crying uncontrollably into trembling hands. For them, the pain of incredible loss was just beginning and a time of uncertainty would close in. It was indeed the end of an era. At this great man's ending, lay an unprotected nation.

Spiritually present at the side of the room, stood a brightly lit and glowing king. He was clothed in an aura of sky blues and purples, at last void of woes and responsibility with a look of pure relief and joy shining out his every pore. Life's contract had been honoured and terminated.

By the raising of his hand he beckoned wee Bruce to join him, and as the boy stepped forward, he touched the youngster's shoulder, transporting him back into the hilltop of the battle.

Positioned in front of the boy was a line of mounted knights, scrutinizing the on-going battle below. In the centre, perched on a wondrous war horse was the king, his gold surcoat ordained by a red rampant lion in all his glory. Beads of sweat squeezed through the chain mailed coif and as the salty water ran into his eye, he refused to falter from his concentration. On his helmet shone a band of gold, sitting perfectly around his forehead and reflecting majestically in the summer sun. Tucked into his belt sat

his axe head, fitted to a new shaft felled from the nearby Torwood. His focus was stuck on the green flats and the Bannock burn below, and as if imitating a lion watching its prey, he never lost his stare for a moment.

As breakthroughs opened below them, knights remarked out loud, shouting out encouragement to their designated squadrons but the king stood firm, not uttering a word, showing no emotion and resolute in his stubbornness to ascend as victor. From below could be heard massed cheers and roars as the engagement reached a peak in the late afternoon. The king's horse stepped forward in anticipation, but only after a stern kick and steel control, this giant animal retraced its steps back into position.

Without warning the King lost his fixed gaze by looking straight at wee Bruce. From his view on high he leaned forward in his saddle and his look was overtaken by puzzlement and wonder. From the side of his mouth appeared a wry smile, followed by a wink of confidence and as the boy welcomed his acceptance, the king pointed to the burn.

As quick as the king's wink, the boy was returned to the battle field below. The battle had come to a conclusion and like all good warring factions locking horns, there were winners and losers. An eerie quietness covered the ground as shadowy figures stripped the bodies of their wealth. There was no emotion or pity for the fallen, this was part and parcel of the hardships of medieval life.

Upon higher ground burned bright orange flames, fed and toasted as celebration bonfires surrounded the area. From the smoke carrying wind, into focus walked the king, investigating and scrutinising the crucible of battle. He showed no signs of sentiment or sympathy as he used his foot as a probe, pushing over fallen enemy.

Suddenly two knights dragged forward a looter, dropping her at his feet. She was an old lady of good age and with hardship etched on her well lined face. She was caught robbing the body of a higher ranking baron, a much prized target of any commander and worthy of chivalric respect. As she begged and cried for forgiveness, her lord and king already on bended knee, stripped the hands of its rings from a fallen faceless contestant, placing them into the woman's hands and sending her on her way.

Every now and then a dark mass of evil spirit would hover around a corpse. These were collectors of bad souls, the evil doers who tortured their fellow man with undesirable punishments upon others below them in the material world. Wee Bruce knew of the dark visitors appearance and purpose, making it a rule not to make eye contact or interfere with their purpose.

Wee Bruce had witnessed the king's kinder nature, now he saw for himself his iron fist. Near to the king rose an enemy knight pretending to be a soldier fallen in battle. Hiding himself under a cloak of cowardice, he'd waited till all fell silent, and using bribery as a bargaining tool, he hoped to trade back his life with gold and jewels.

"Good king," he began, "I noticed the regal generosity and pity you poured upon the old stinking hag reeking with disease, and obviously not of good stock as you or I."
He brandished his ring filled fingers to the king.
"These will surely enrich your life and fill your money chests, and with good faith, Sire, I shall part with these objects like old friends and un-wanted turds, and no more shall be said of this matter and favours I have presented you with."
His teeth chatted as if a seller selling cheap meat at a local farmers market.
"May I assure you sire that the back biting rumours spoken of you are false indeed. I have listened to great detail in our camp of how you are portrayed as a simple thief, arsonist of ancient antiquity and killer of men in holy places to mention a few."

The king listened intensely but said nothing - yet.
The enemy soldier continued.

"I understand you are a man of substance, and generosity and stories of your leniency are rife around my king's great table, and of course he speaks of you well, and no doubt if you were to return with me to his palace he would find it in his gracious heart to forgive your traitor acts of abomination against his most holy crown. On my journey home on a good steed donated by your good self, I shall inform the king of your greatness and I have no doubt you will be welcomed into his fold and furnished with further prizes only found in the best of dreams."

The king spoke, in a clear calm voice.
"Your promises of a heavenly life please me indeed good knight, to hold me in favour with your great lord and king is a deed only a fool would relinquish; and with your honest conduct, minions of many must have bowed to your great wealth. But I must inform you, good Sir, that on this occasion I shall hold the title of thief as spoken at the dinner table of your said nobles, for I shall take what was stolen and return to my people what was theirs in the first place. To even the old hag, stinking of disease, this land is hers and it is also her heritage to do with as she pleases."

Then from a simple nod to a general, the enemy soldier's body was bereft of its head and was immediately accompanied away by a dark mass of evil spirit. On the ground lay two hands of very fine jewellery indeed, free for the picking. Two crows had the last word as dinner was served.

From across the far side of the grassland, a cheer went up from the camp followers or 'small folk' as they were called. These people had few valuables at all in life and bordered mostly on the brink of hunger. However, on this day they sat swamped in clean linens and warm furs, drinking wines and fine ales from silver goblets. These goods had been transported in wagons by arrogant men with arrogant attitudes of domination. The fires burnt with the overpowering smell of horse meat, enough food to fill their empty bellies for an eternity. For their hardship and struggles, they were allowed that privilege.

As the king turned and disappeared back into the smoke, the wind caught his cloak, flapping it upwards to his shoulder, escorting him on his way. With one quick backwards glance the king vanished into the history books, proclaiming his prize of freedom, but at a very heavy cost to all who lay on the day's blood soaked fields.

A sharp poke to wee Bruce's ribs alerted him. He was sure he'd been targeted by a bowman, he felt for an entry wound made by an arrowhead but there was none. His eyes opened and he was in bed, his brother Edward was poking him awake to come downstairs as breakfast was

served. It took him longer in getting dressed, movements were slow and his mind was still full with vivid images, making it hard to concentrate.

It was times like this when the boy was silent at the table, his dream-like experiences whizzing around his head, trying to remember all that was shown to him. Others at the table would stare at him, they knew it was very unusual for him to be so quiet and wondered if he was perhaps ill.

The boy understood; it was a vision given to him to

prepare for the future, so he never questioned it. Yet inside somewhere deep he knew he would follow the same path. This was the way of the warrior and to survive he would have, sometime in his life, to put his hand to learning this despicable trade of combat.

He never wanted to fight, but he was born into an era when fighting was a necessary survival tool, and dangers would always be lurking around the corner in every part of his growing up.

"You look tired," said his mother, "Looks like you've been in a battle."

THE END

3.
MAID
by Paul V Hunter

Maid

Loch Lomond is the jewel of Scottish lochs. Its natural beauty and wildlife is surpassed by none, carved out from the last ice age and split in half by a mountainous fault line. From a winter morning to a summer evening its mystic beauty beggars belief, possessing and embracing secrets from as far back as prehistoric times.

The dark waters are permanently stocked with salmon, trout, giant eels, water kelpies, pike, otters and on surrounding dry land by pine martens, bears, red deer, beavers, badgers, fox and wild boar. A true nature's menagerie indeed.

It was a mild afternoon as a gentle summer breeze ran from behind Ben Lomond down Loch Lomond and finally settling at Balloch, where the River Leven meets the Loch. Boats from around the area assembled together for the annual competition to land the biggest salmon. The much sought after prize was a year's tax free fishing for the winner, and all who took part retained their heaviest catch as a runner-up prize. The challenge itself reeled in fishermen from all over the parish of Cardross, young and old, as wee Bruce sat at the starboard side of his father's friend's boat named 'The Abigail'. Its flour white sail was in full view, guided and steered by the wind. He wasn't planning to stand up as on two occasions he nearly fell over due to the wet greasy walking boards upon the boat. Just as the boat left the Leven entering the loch, a loud grinding sound was heard from beneath the hull.

"What was that?" asked the boy.

"That's Mirren," answered the captain steering the craft.

The boy's inquisitive nature probed onward.

"What's Mirren?" asked the youngster.

"Mirren is the name of the village that was carried forcibly down to damnation under the loch never to be seen again; a disaster so terrible, most folks refuse to converse about it for fear of provoking the dead that roam under these deep dark waters," said the captain crossing himself.

"What made that sound, father?" asked the boy, looking for confirmation.

The captain turned, facing wee Bruce, "That, my boy, is an utterance from the church steeple scraping the underside of The Abigail. The village is preserved there with the people trapped in their houses never to be recovered. No diver or fisherman ever fishes here due to bad luck and a curse befalls the boat who does. The sound you hear is a reminder to all to heed the warnings and every time there's a strong current, the bell to this day rings, stirring the inhabitants awake."

The boy's father wasn't taking it too seriously as he laughed, nudging the captains shoulder.

"I wish I could see it," remarked the boy.

"Be careful what you ask for," said his father.

The captain continued, "It is said that sirens, evil mermaids, who smash ships onto the rocks in bad weather, jealously guard the dead as they sleep, till one day when the loch completely freezes over, they will ascend again from the deep dark depths of a hundred to six hundred feet, gaining their vengeance by hauling beneath all the children they can get their scaly webbed hands on."

The boy became quiet for a spell and moved away a little from the edge, eyeballs wide and staring intensively into the dark murky waters. To one side of the boat at the shore was the ancestral home of the Earls of Lennox, protected by a motte and standing out of the water to the other side was Monkey Island, so named after a holy man who brought a monkey with him from the Holy Land and settled on the island. It is said the monkey was eventually captured and eaten by poor starving locals, and every now and then the angry creature's little ghost can be heard chatting its teeth as it swings through the trees looking for its master.

As the river waters collided with the loch current, an unexpected wave impacted with the side of the boat causing her to tip steeply, launching all the occupants against the heavy wooden sides. Cups, plates and fishing tackle were flung about, smashing and hitting the occupants. A box packed with lead weights flew off the table top emptying its contents, aiming one at wee Bruce's head and knocking him to the floor. Another strong wave battered into the boat once more, tipping it over completely throwing the whole crew overboard. It was all over in a flash. Bubbles – muffled, gargled un-audible voices shrieking and a nostril filling force mixed with frenzied disorder and bewildering cold sensations. A debauched puzzlement swell of watery panic swallowed by gluttonous grasping gulps. Then a motionless silence. A splitting giddy headache revived the boy from a disturbing day dream.

He opened his eyes but darkness remained. He was cold and shivering as the fresh air filled his lungs. It felt good. He was experiencing the sensation of being wrapped in someone's arms, so he waited a little, enjoying the attention and body warmth. He was aware of his legs in water, dropping in temperature from the rest of his body and he wished to warm his feet. It was then a hand touched his face, unveiling a cloth from his eyes and letting in blinding bright sunlight.

He found himself lying by the shore but not on the rough shingle. Instead he was placed on the lap of the most beautiful girl he could ever imagine. Looking down on him was a curly white haired heavenly vision with larger than normal green heart piercing eyes with the largest pupils and flowered lips painted with bluebells. Her cheeks were decorated with two red circles, shaped as if with natural sponge and surrounded by a covering of the finest cutest freckles. He didn't notice any ears as her hair covered them.

The boy's lips shook from the cold. "Can you take my legs out of the water, they're cold?" he asked.

"You'll have to walk out yourself, I can come no farther," she answered looking to the direction of her feet, as did wee Bruce. She lifted her lower half enough to be seen out the water exposing her fish-like scaled fins where her legs and feet should be.

The boy pulled his legs onto dry land. "You're a fish?" he asked.

She smiled. "I've been called many names, some not so nice," she answered. "I don't mind the usage of mermaid, that's a popular one around here."

Looking around he asked, "Where's my father's boat?"

She placed a hand on the boys shoulder. "Don't worry he's safe."

The boy closed his knees together for warmth. "How did you know I was in the water, was it you and your kind who sunk my father's friend's boat?"

"My kind don't sink boats," she answered, "And anyway I heard your wish from on-board the boat that you wanted to see the old village under the loch."

"You heard that?" asked the boy surprised.

"Of course," she said, "We've existed here for tens of thousands of years, we hear everything connected to the loch, even your thoughts. We are the guardians of Loch

Lomond and surrounding islands and sometimes we grant wishes."

The boy pointed out towards the water, "Can you show me the village of Mirren?"
"Only if you really want to but you must keep it a secret?" she answered.
"I'm good at keeping secrets," he said, "You can trust me."
She placed her hand on his chest and said the word 'Mirren'.

He didn't remember falling asleep but he awoke at the top of Balloch hill way above the Earl of Lennox's castle. In his site was a spectacular panoramic view of Loch Lomond, Monkey Island and further up at the old Viking settlement of Midross. Directly across the water at Cameron point was located an old house and just up the hill the site of the ancient burial tombs bequeathed by Iron Age man. Lower down past Monkey Island and standing above the water line was a piece of green flat land occupied by a village of substantial buildings and farms. This was the village of Mirren named after the island Inchmirren on the loch. From his vantage point he could make out movement of people, herds of cattle, running horses and see the smoke belching from local fires. There must have been a fair, as a good crowd was gathered around the middle of the village and away in the distance he could hear faint cheering.

The loch was calm and the clouds were high enough,
pulling the gulls towards them, making it the perfect day
for a fair. It was very picturesque and the surrounding lands
shone in all nature's beauty and glory. There was no better
place in the world and God indeed had made an Eden
on Earth. At the beginning of the village was the church,
situated as the first building when entering the village, its
proud steeple stretching out high above the other houses,
its people emptying from its doors as the chimes from its
bells reached the boys' ears as he sat perched above the hill.

From under the ground where the boy was seated, came
a rumble. He placed his hands on the grass, feeling its
vibration as it repeated the motion, it sounded like thunder.

The birds flew away in all directions and the village dogs barked continuously. What was happening?

All of a sudden the whole hillside shook with an enormous force, enough to snap branches clean from the trees. Wee Bruce was alarmed. He stood up but was forced back down again losing his balance to the violent shaking. He wanted to hold onto something but there was nothing but grass, so he lay on his belly and waited. Below in the village the locals began running out of their homes coming together in groups. A massive explosion sound seemed to emit from inside Ben Lomond, crashing all its surrounding forest into the loch causing an almighty splash and show of white water as it entered. Wee Bruce covered his eyes for a few seconds, he was feeling giddy as the ground shook and his legs were trembling. The boy then watched helplessly as a huge chunk of mountainside slipped away from Ben Lomond, disappearing into the deep dark chasm, throwing the water hundreds of feet up into the air.

The sound of the rock hitting the loch could be heard for miles as it fell noisily into the watery depths like stampeding oxen. This was followed by another earth shake, this one larger, battering the Loch Lomond area from side to side. By this point the boy was on all fours as it seemed to be the safest place to be at the time.

From below, a good part of the population had made it to the church, cramming themselves inside. Cattle and horses were spooked and had broken free from their harnesses, riding roughshod through the village. It was pandemonium. On the opposite side of the loch from the boy, landslides were dragging trees on a trip from the top of the hill to the bottom and fishing boats had escaped their moorings, jumping around erratically, taking in water. Several massive holes in the ground had opened up, spewing mud into the loch and local blacksmith sheds were being swallowed up where they stood. Huge ancient pine trees were swaying dramatically and sparring with smaller trees, snapping and knocking them to the ground.

A huge number of birds had flocked together flying over the boy's head escaping the turmoil. The birds were the lucky ones.

Locals lit torched arrows which they fired into the air to attract help from neighbouring villages or passers by but it was to no avail. No help came or was to come. As wee Bruce observed the final piece of falling rock from the mountain disappear into the bubbling waters, the height of the loch rose twenty feet into the air resembling a castle wall. Then with the feeling of a twisting knot in his stomach he watched as the wall of water began its journey towards Balloch and the village of Mirren. In the distance its sickening roar sounded like armoured cavalry, a million strong charging their way to battle. As if this wasn't enough, nature gave a final shake, a last small shudder but enough to feed the humongous water wall, giving a final push towards its target.

Then something strange happened. The villagers awaited their demise by stopping, each lit a torch and stood outside facing the enormous wave. Every man, women and child stood motionless, facing this destructive power of nature as if accepting their fate. The wave of destruction reached half way towards the village as the boy glanced to his side, something moving caught his eye. It was a butterfly. It flapped it wings at half the normal speed, every moment in

sequence and with nothing rushed.

Out of the chaos bloomed a carefree gentle abundance of simple, subtle life. This flying flower of fancy moved amongst the grasses and summer flowers, lost in its own being, immune and absent to man's world and void of care and worry. Its unique creation of function was to intermingle with all that was good in nature's miniature silent world, dancing as light as air itself, reminding man of the abundance of untapped wonder in the world. Its colours were indescribable, unattainable to man's superficial pallet, portraying its angel form in feeding desire to universal curiosity.

Such things were surely placed to lessen man's burden in his world. As wee Bruce thought to touch, it fluttered off as if understanding the temptation to own. Its secret for now would remain intact and its lace frame focused the boy's thoughts to the distance where his eyes caught the attention of a dark marine giant striding towards Mirren. As the water mass grew louder the people held hands, singing their hearts out a long forgotten song of unity and meaning, the words mattered not as the show of togetherness stood out for all to see. Their actions embodied the meaning of community and spirit and there would be none to sustain dignity like them again.

The noise level rose to a deafening rumble, amplified by high pitched collision impacts as the brown muddy world came down on the village. The water hammered and crushed with ease everything that stood upright, brushing aside all signs of life and its earth and water mixture surfed scores of lifeless fish caught up in the melee. The village of Mirren was no more.

Wee Bruce was left at his high vantage point pondering the destruction of a people. He thought of the mermaid and immediately began choking. Pressure, coldness, muffled splashes and earache. Dark light confusion then his lungs filled with water. As he gulped at the fresh air the boy opened his eyes and lying on the shore line was his father and friends coughing, dragging each other onto dry land.

The boy lay on dry shingle, he was safe. All around them other boats had come to their assistance, making sure all had made it safely out of the water. It wasn't unusual for a boat to capsize on the loch during a competition but wee Bruce never thought it would be his turn. Neither did he think that deep under the water someone listened into his thoughts and would grant his wish in such a mysterious manner. In the future he would be careful what he wished for as it was shown it can come true. In the meantime, the skipper of the boat sat up looking in the direction to where the boat went down.

"Looks like you nearly got your wish young Bruce. The mermaids and sirens didn't want us on the loch today and overturned our boat."

"Mermaids don't overturn boats," replied the boy, "They're the keepers of the loch."

"We definitely hit the steeple," said his father.

"We did that," said the boy, "That's exactly where it is."

As the day came to an end, the sun disappeared over the horizon, the loch inherited an orange haze covering the area with a wonderful warm glow, matched by the smells of trees, heathers and grasses. Even the loch itself smelled of life, buzzing flies, dragonflies and swifts skimmed the still mirrored surface filling up on their summer feast. There could have been no calmer vision or dreamlike Eden quality to the loch and many a Celtic oracle has praised the mystic sanctuary of Loch Lomond, proclaiming it to be God's own designed garden on Earth. Less known and understood is the weary dreamer who confuses nature's will with sentiment. She will always have the last word for she is unpredictable and self destructive; she is stunning yet unforgiving in her devastation and slaughter of beautiful things we mortals hold dear. Be careful what you wish for.

THE END

4.
FEVER
by Paul V Hunter

Fever

Wee Bruce was ill. He'd been flat out in bed for nearly a week. For the last few days it was just a matter of drifting in and out of a deep sleep and days were passing without him noticing. Blinding headaches and fever were too much for him, rendering him a small bundle wrapped up in his father's bed surrounded by rows and rows of candles. The pox had been doing its rounds and rumours started weeks ago regarding a flu type virus sweeping across western Scotland. It was said to have come from a visiting ship sailing in from the Holy Land, arriving at nearby Dumbarton harbour by the castle. The local people said it

was a sign from God, cleansing all the wickedness and sin
from all the land. His mother assured him it was nothing
of the sort and would pass after a week. Apart from that,
he was too ill to care anyway where it came from. Night
was really terrible for him. Bouts of dizziness and sore eyes
plagued him all through the darkness. The only time it left
him was when the 'visitors' came. They were a group of
bizarre characters that would occupy the space at the foot
of his bed, jabbering joking gibberish for hours. He didn't
recognise them nor had he seen them at the manor house,
and he certainly would have remembered this strange
assortment of figures.

He awoke. He'd just realised he was sleeping and it annoyed him. He was overtired and because he was snoozing so much, getting back to sleep was proving more difficult. Something caught his eye. There were two small figures sitting or leaning in the corner beside the chair.
"Why don't you sit on the chair?" he asked.
"We don't need a chair," came the reply.

He then demanded,
"Then come closer so I can see you."
The figures approached wee Bruce, resting their arms on the end of the bed. He was then very surprised at the fact they were not two figures but five!

He was even more surprised to learn that they were not sitting but standing.
"How come you're so small?"
A little voice answered him,
"How come you're so tall?"

The boy didn't answer. His eyes were fixed on their clothes. Two of them looked like miniature Vikings, gripping onto double headed axes that needed two hands to hold the weight. Two others resembled chain-mailed armour clad warriors, clasping short swords fastened to their sides. The last one, who was just a shade taller than the rest, wore the look of the leader. He had a beard and wore a piece of tartan wrapped around his forehead. Dangling down his back attached to coloured rope was an array of silver buckles. He spoke.

"You feeling any better, son?"

The boy, staring at the ceiling, replied, "I feel terrible, can't hardly move a muscle."

"My name is Guy," said the leader, "this is Orlam, Frieda, Chelta and Max."

"Frieda?" he asked surprised, "You're a girl?"

Frieda bullied her way to the front.

"I am. I'm a girl, so what? I'll fight you if you want?"

The other four covered her mouth with their hands, pushing her to the back of the group.

"No Frieda, I don't want to fight you," replied the boy, "anyway, how come you know me, I've never seen you before?"

Chelta answered, "Oh yes you have, you have seen us many times. You have spoken to us before in the dark hours of the night."

The boy rubbed his sore eyes.

"How did you get into the mansion without being seen?"

"You always ask us that, good Sir," replied Orlam.

"I don't remember asking you anything," said wee Bruce.

Frieda stepped forward and whispered,

"You summoned us here through your thoughts, don't you
remember?"

Taking his hands away from his eyes he said,
"So you're not real then, it's only my imagination?"
"Oh, we're real alright as you'll find out," laughed Orlam.
"You asked us to come, we appear and go to where ever
you want us to take you, good Sir. Where would you like to
go this time?"
"It's difficult for me to go anywhere," he said, "My bones
and muscles are aching. I can't even move my legs."

"Move them now," said Max.

It was then the youngster moved his arms upwards without strain or pain. The soreness was gone and this time he lost the feeling of faint when he sat up. His body felt really light and the heaviness that anchored him to his bed had gone. He couldn't believe it. Pulling back the fur covers he arose and walked over to the window.

Outside was pitch black, broken by flies of bright burning balls of light in the distance from the lit torches sparked by his father's guards. The boy wondered again how his visitors managed to penetrate the security guards. Then something wonderful happened. A thought came into his head. He imagined himself sitting on a huge stallion wading through fields and rivers. The room spun horribly with stomach turning swaying and head throbbing pressure, sucking his brain through his skull like never before...FLASH!

To his astonishment he was outside. The bright sun was beating on his neck and the scent of every essence filled his lungs. It was very warm; too warm to enjoy. He was seated on a whiter than white wacky stallion, standing knee deep in the river. The river was so clear, baggy minnows swam around the horse's hooves and he could spot every pebble resting on the river bottom. Lazing near the riverbank was his five little companions, relaxed and dangling their fishing

nets in the water.

"Caught anything?" he asked.

Chelta removed a large bramble from between his teeth.

"Nah, we never do."

Just then, a voice echoed from the other side of the river,

"That'll be my brambles you're eating Chelta."

His new friends sat up and huddled closer to each other as

if alerted to some danger. "It's anybody's brambles," replied

Chelta.

"That's right, and I'll fight you for them," shouted Frieda.

It was a mysterious woman leaning on a staff made of yew tree. From under a humongous hat she revealed beady eyes and a nose fit for warts. "You know the law about eating someone else's brambles?"

"It's only a wee bramble," said Guy.

"Shut your neck!" demanded the old woman. "Let's see what King Robert has to say about it?"

Wee Bruce had a long good stare at the old woman. He sensed there was no hint of kindness at all from her and she was bent on making trouble. His plan was to stay calm, trying his best not to provoke her. Anyway, what harm could come from an old woman depending on a walking stick? He put on his diplomatic voice he heard his father use at meetings, "You say 'the law' regarding eating someone else's brambles. Whose law?"

Placing her hand near her hat, she replied, "My law."

Sewn onto her hat was a huge brown button. The boy had never seen a button so large. Who would need a button this size? For what purpose would this huge button have? Was it from a gigantic pair of trousers? Was it from an enormous shirt? What size of thread could tie such a button? Then, without warning, she touched the button with her hand making poor little Chelta vanish. WOOSH! He was gone. Frightened, Max, Orlam, Frieda and Guy re-grouped, moving closer to each other, throwing their fishing nets into the water and huddling close for safety.

"As I said," groaned the old woman. "My law."
Bramble nettles from the nearby bush began gliding along the ground like horrible grabbing hands, sliding across the grass to where the small people were. They grappled onto the others' legs, picking them up and dangling them in the air. As the group were plucked up one by one they desperately attempted to hold onto the ground but the branches were too powerful. They each screamed in fear as they were swung about like a child's toy, the dizziness was terrible and they begged for it to cease.

The brambles themselves exploded from within, revealing blood and splattered ooze everywhere. Wee Bruce prayed to be back at the house. The room fell high out of control, toppling down a spiral shaft, falling forever from a great dizzy height, squeezing his head to a pulp...FLASH!

He was back in his kitchen at the manor house, surrounded by the other four placed at the dinner table. On the table in front of them sat six meals fit for a king. The heat in the kitchen was stifling. It was very warm.
"You feeling any better, good Sir?" asked Orlam.
"Just a wee bit confused," replied the boy, "Where's Chelta?"

Max had his face dug deep into his plate,

"Mmm, never tasted food so good."

"Tuck in folks, I'm starving," said Guy.

"But what about Chelta?" he repeated.

"Aren't you hungry, son?" asked Orlam, throwing fistfuls of food into his mouth. The boy had not eaten for three days. He'd trouble keep it down, and anyway, he'd lost his appetite due to the sickness feeling in his stomach. Part of his bed sheet still exhibited the evidence of sick stains as he threw up near to his pillows the night before. He noticed the kitchen looked a little weird. He'd only visited the kitchen a handful of times, receiving a snack before his dinner from 'toothless Mary', the house cook. On the walls, knives and forks were dangling all over the place as if someone had used them for target practice. Three legged chairs with shoes on, around six feet high were stacked up in every corner. And strange still, there was no ceiling and no roof. Above their heads floated white puffy clouds backed with a deep blue sky. The entrance door was long and slant and it opened out the way instead of in, and squeezing through poured out a very bushy moustached man dressed in a white cloak. He wore a gravy and blood stained apron, chaperoned with a white saggy hat, topped with a huge brown button sewn into the middle. His hanging chubby fat bottom lip wobbled as he saw his guests sitting at the table.

Confused, the boy asked, "You're not toothless Mary?"
"Shut your neck!" demanded the cook. "Who said you could eat my food?"
"Well, there's six meals served and there's six of us," said Max, almost choking on a well-stacked cow rib.

The cook dried wet slobber hanging from his bottom lip, throwing it onto the table.
"By whose authority do you have to eat here?" he shouted.
"By whose authority?" demanded wee Bruce, "this is my father's house. Who are you? I've never seen you before and what happened to the roof? Why do the chairs have legs missing and why are the knives and forks stuck into the walls?"

The cook raised his four fat flat flavoured fingers resembling a pig's trotter, touching the huge brown button on his white saggy hat. WOOSH! Max vanished. His half eaten meat rib fell to the floor. Just then, a mouse with a pig's head ran out of a hole in the wall, grabbing the rib and scurrying back again. Frieda, Guy and Orlam dropped their plates and ran to the back door trying to escape. The back door was false. It was just a painted image on the wall. They screamed in panic as the forks came off the wall, flying around the room sticking into things. The clouds from above then dropped into the kitchen, floating above their heads, soaking them with rain and hail. To protect himself from the flying missiles, the boy dived quickly under the table, at the same time putting his hands over his ears to dim the panic screams.

It was then he thought about the safety of the forest. The room exploded inside out with a terrible pulling of gravity, the interior body blood becoming lead weight heavy crushing his head ... FLASH!

He found himself lying under a tree shaded from the sun. Blue tits and chaffinches were singing their hearts out as Guy, Frieda and Orlam jumped into the air waving long sticks at over hanging delicious ripe apples. He was grateful for being under the tree, as it was very warm and he was aware of beads of sweat running down his face.

"You feeling any better, good Sir?" asked Orlam. "Not sure," he replied, "I'm a wee bit confused, it's very hot."
"You help yourself to one of these," said Guy, throwing a large red apple in the thirsty boy's direction. He caught it with one hand and bit into it.

It was succulent, juicy, sweet and most importantly, wet. Although he chomped into it and felt the juices run down the back of his throat, he still had an enormous thirst and no matter how much apple he ate, his thirst wouldn't leave him. "Where's Max?" he asked.

"If we could climb to the top of the tree we could reach the much larger apples," said Guy.

"Tell you what", said Frieda. "I'm the smallest. Why don't you throw me into the air towards the top of the tree, I'll land on the top branch and throw down the apples?"

"Good idea," said Guy, "let's do it."

The boy remained in the shade, raising his hands to shade his eyes, watching the others trying to reach the top. Orlam and Guy stood at the base, their hands presented together almost like a step made from fingers.

Frieda sprinted from twenty yards towards them. He couldn't believe how her little legs could move so fast. She reached Orlam and Guy. Their hands catapulted her up to the air with ease, making her crash into the top branch, knocking dozens of apples to the ground. Orlam and Guy cheered loudly. Wee Bruce applauded, laughing at the same time, as he couldn't believe what he'd just witnessed. An apple landed on his head causing him pain and discomfort.

Just then, two young girls appeared and stopped to look up at Frieda. They were twins. They were identical and nobody could tell them apart. They each wore jute sackcloth as clothes and were bare footed. Joining them together from belly button height was a huge brown button sewn between their costume.

"Hello," said the boy trying to be nice.

"We are six and seven," answered the girls together.

"I thought you were twins? " he remarked

"We are," said the girls, "That's our names"

"That's strange names, who gave you them?" he asked.

"I hope you're not eating the green apples?" they said.

"There are not green apples, only red," replied Frieda.

The girls stepped forward, "If you find any green ones you must give us them," warned the twins.

He looked to the ground at the fallen apples; they were all red.

"If you find a green one you know what will happen?" said the twins.

"We're not going to be told off by a couple of young girls," said Guy, "Go away or I'll bounce an apple of your heads."

"You'd better run along," the boy said trying to be diplomatic again, "Your mother will be looking for you both."

It was then the twins placed their hands on the huge brown button connecting them. One by one the apples fell from the tree. Intrigued, wee Bruce stepped back for a better look. Guy and Orlam, began screaming as if being attacked by wasps. Again, he couldn't believe his eyes as to what he was witnessing. Not only did the apples turn green, they each had eyes and razor sharp teeth. As they were landing on Orlam and Guy, they were biting them on the head, neck, shoulders and arms. They both ran off screaming, trying to tear dozens of attacking apples from their heads and jumping into the nearby river to escape, sinking to the bottom and disappearing.

The boy was horrified. An apple smashed into the side of his head. Another one, two, three walloped his face knocking him to the ground. He couldn't open his eyes for the pain and he could hear the apples ganging up on him. The noise of teeth gnashing against each other became louder and louder. He wished he had a boat. His head grew three times the size, exploding with three times the pressure, an immense frightening pull on his balance spun out of control ... FLASH!

He found himself on a small fishing boat. He watched as bushes and trees painted by every kind of green in the world passed by his point of view. He watched as a striped bumblebee flew close to his nose, stuck its tongue out and flew upwards out of sight. He lifted his head. Steering the boat was Frieda.

"Did we get Orlam and Guy?" he asked.

"You feeling any better?" asked Frieda.

His neck was soaked with sweat, it was very warm.

"Where's the apples?" he asked.

"Don't you just love boats?" asked Frieda. "The feeling of floating around forever, watching the world going by. If I had a hundred boats I'd take over the world, I'd fight the largest of armies and rule the waves."

"Why do you always want to fight all the time?" asked the boy.

Frieda replied, "I can become the most powerful queen in the country, everyone will fear me and I'll be the greatest ruler of all time, wearing the most beautiful of dresses and the most expensive jewels. Are you hungry? I have delicious mushrooms in my pouch. Here, try one."

Throwing it at wee Bruce, he caught it in his mouth without using his hands. It was delicious. Soaked in herbs and spices, breaking up easily in his mouth, making it easy to swallow. But one wasn't enough and he was very thirsty.

"Do you have any water?" his dry lips asked.

"No, sorry," said Frieda, "Just mushrooms."

A shout came from the other side of the river.

"It's my water."

"Who said that?" shouted Frieda.

"Get your boat off my water!" screamed the voice again.

"Show yourself whoever you are!" replied the boy.

From the riverbank stood what resembled a stick with
a small mouth. As the boat reached the embankment it
appeared to be a snake standing up on end.

"I've never seen a snake speak before," remarked the boy.
"I've seen lots of things, but not this."

"No-one ever sailed a boat on my water before," answered
the snake.

The boy sighed, "Seems as though everyone owns
everything around here today."

The snake answered with a huge lisp. "All I know is that
I own the water and you should not be polluting it with
your filthy boat."

"Don't tell me," said the boy, "you're going to spit poison at
us?"

"No," replied the snake, "I already poisoned the
mushrooms."

The boy felt panic in his chest. Already he began to feel
weird, his eyes were getting heavy and he was beginning
to lose control. He could see Frieda calling out to him but
he couldn't hear or help her. He could see other snakes
standing up and throwing themselves like spears towards
her. One hit her on the head, knocking her completely out
of the boat into the water. One of her hands gripped onto
the boat and she was screaming at him to save her from
drowning. Suddenly the sky got dark and the air filled with

the smell of rotten eggs. Wee Bruce couldn't move, his body was heavy and he couldn't lift a hand to help her.

Red hailstones began falling from the sky, swelling up the boat with water. Before his eyes sealed completely shut, his last vision was seeing more snake spears slashing on Frieda's hand, forcing her to let go, slipping into the deep water. The boy couldn't fight it anymore. His eyeballs rolled to close, sinking him into a deep sleep and he was floating … floating in space. His body was weightless and glided into the air as if tied to an invisible cord, dragging him all over the place. Around him he was aware of whispers and they became louder until the whisper spoke as voice he recognised calling his name.

"Robert." Slowly he opened his eyes. "Robert." He was back in his room. He was lying in bed with a wet cloth over his forehead. His mother was leaning over him and his father stood in the background looking over.
"Welcome back," said his mother, "Your fever has broken, you're on the mend now."

His mother and father then left the room, closing the door behind them. A fresh breeze blew through the opened window messing his hair … it was a wonderful feeling. He noticed to the side of his bed stood a small table. On it sat a bowl of brambles, a cup of water, a plate of fresh mushrooms and two red shiny apples. Next to the bowl was one loose brown button that came off his pyjamas. Just to make sure, he looked around the room for any small characters lurking about looking for an adventure. There was no-one to be seen. It was good to be back.

THE END

Paul Victor Hunter

Paul was born in Robroyston, Glasgow in 1962 shortly before his twin sister Donna.

He studied Media and Communication at Clydebank College in Scotland and is an award winning short film maker through his writing and as an actor. Paul also studies Scottish history and culture, and participates in living history events. Inspired by the 19th century fairytales and folklore created in Germany by the Brothers Grimm, Paul has branched into writing childrens' fictional short stories and poetry.

As a younger man, Paul spent several years as a fashion model, before moving to Belgium. There, he lived the bohemian life style as an artist for seven years with exhibitions in Antwerp and Brussels. He speaks Flemish and Dutch.

At an early age Paul obtained the gift of spiritualism and has used these psychic experiences to write his 'Wee Bruce' short stories. They focus on a 'gifted' boy who accepts his fate during the medieval period, and through hardships is helped and influenced through the spirit world.

Anne Marshall

Anne was born in Dumbarton in 1956 and is the youngest of six children. She always loved to draw and paint and was delighted to be given the opportunity to illustrate this book.

Anne lives in the shadow of Dumbarton Castle, which she has sketched and painted many times. Anne has three grown up children and four grandchildren for whom she has written and illustrated a book after many requests to 'tell us about the olden days'.

Anne spends a lot of time at 'The Hub' in Dumbarton where she displays her work and enjoys the company of other artists. She is seen here with the author and the publisher of this book.

Catherine Crome

Catherine was born in Boston, Lincolnshire on a very special date – the second day of the second month of the second year. She moved to Scotland with her sister, Eleanor (seen here) and mum, Sarah, in 2011.

Catherine quickly made friends at her new school, but her life was soon turned upside down when she was diagnosed with Ewing's Sarcoma, a rare form of cancer at the age of 11. Her lengthy treatment at Yorkhill Hospital, Glasgow has been very successful and she has shown immense courage throughout.

Catherine loves art, playing computer games, hill walking, archery and watching movies.

OTHER TITLES FROM AUCH BOOKS.....
From Greek author Konstantina Ritsou

'The Boy and the Well of Memory' is by Greek author Konstantina Ritsou. For the first time it tells the story of Andrew de Moray, joint Guardian of Scotland with William Wallace and co-commander of the victorious Battle of Stirling Bridge. RRP £11.99. Visit our website to find out more, where you can also buy the book.

'Looking for William', also by Greek author Konstantina Ritsou, is a theatrical composition from Shakespeare's texts. It is an engaging take on the life and times of William Shakespeare. RRP £9.99. Visit our website to find out more, where you can also buy the book.